You Read to Me, I'll Read to You

Very Short Stories to Read Together

by
MARY ANN HOBERMAN

Illustrated by
MICHAEL EMBERLEY

Megan Tingley Books

 Little, Brown and Company
Boston New York London

First Edition

Library of Congress Cataloging-in-Publication Data

Hoberman, Mary Ann.
    You read to me, I'll read to you / by Mary Ann Hoberman ; illustrated by Michael
Emberley. — 1st ed.
        p. cm.
    ISBN 0-316-14544-0
        1. Children's poetry, American. [1. Books and reading — Poetry. 2. American poetry.]
    I. Emberley, Michael, ill. II. Title.
    PS3558.O3367 Y68 2001
    811'.54 — dc21   00-035230

10 9 8 7 6 5 4 3 2 1

TWP

Printed in Singapore

The illustrations for this book were done in ballpoint pen, watercolor, and dry pastel on 90-lb.
hot-press watercolor paper.
The text was set in Horley Old Style, and the display type is Shannon.

Author's Note:

It's fun to read aloud! It's fun to read together! Each short, rhymed story in this book is like a little play for two voices. Sometimes the voices are separate; sometimes they speak in unison. The stories are about all kinds of things: cats and puppies, bears and mice, snakes, telephones, snowmen, birthdays, friendships, and more. But no matter what their subject, they all finish with a variation on the same refrain:

> *You read to me!*
> *I'll read to you!*

My work with Literacy Volunteers of America provided inspiration for both the format and the purpose of this book, which is to promote literacy by reading to, and listening to, each other. I envision the book's users as either a pair of beginning readers (two children, or a child and a parent who is in a literacy program) or one beginning and one more-advanced reader (either an older child or an adult). In other words, everyone who loves to read!

To my colleagues at Literacy Volunteers of America,
Stamford/Greenwich Chapter

—M. A. H.

For Evelyn Emberley
1911–2000
Who never stopped kidding around

—M. E.

Introduction

Here's a book
With something new —

You read to me!

I'll read to you!

We'll read each page
To one another —

You'll read one side,

I the other.

But who will read —
Now guess this riddle —
When the words are
In the middle?

The answer's easy!

Plain as pie!

We'll read together,
You and I.

The Two Mice

I see a mouse.

        I see one, too!

We see two mice.
What shall we do?

Let's give them names.

        What shall they be?

Pipe and Peep?

        He and She?

Dot and Dash?

        Squeal and Squeak?

To and Fro?

        Hide and Seek?

Two mice are nice.

   Two mice are fun.

They're twice as nice

   As only one.

And when we read,

   It's just the same.

Two readers reading

   Make a game.

It's twice as nice

   When there are two.

 You read to me.
 I'll read to you.

The Big Cat

Oh my, I spy
A great big cat!

A great big cat?
I don't like that!

Run, mice, run!

Stay, cat, stay!

Oh, good, the mice
Have got away!

Now, pussycat,
That isn't nice.
You shouldn't scare
The little mice.

We know you want them
For your food
But eating mice
Is really rude.

It's not a proper
Thing to do.
Why, what if someone
Gobbled you?

Think how sad
Your friends would feel
If *you* were eaten
For a meal.

We'll give you cream,
Your very own,
If you will leave
The mice alone.

And when you're done
And full and fat,
We'll find a book
About a cat,

A cat like you
With fluffy fur
Who laps up cream
And loves to purr

And lives inside
A little house
And never ever
Dines on mouse.

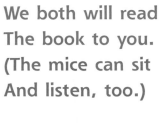

We both will read
The book to you.
(The mice can sit
And listen, too.)

I Hate My Hat

I hate my hat!

    I think it's nice.

I hate my hat!

    You've said that twice.

I hate my hat!

    Now that's a third.

I hate my hat!

    I hate that word!

You hate that word?
What word is that?

    That word you said.

You mean my hat?

    No, not your hat!
    Your hat looks great.
    I like your hat.
    It's "hate" I hate.

But not my hat?
You don't hate that?

    Of course I don't.
    I like your hat.

You like my hat?

> I said I do.
> I think your hat
> Looks good on you.

You like my hat?

> I like it fine.
> I like your hat.
> Do you like mine?

Why, yes, I do.
It suits your head.
Now let's do something
Else instead.

> Something else
> We both would like.

Let's wear our hats
And ride a bike.

> That sounds good.
> We'll take a snack.

What should we do
When we get back?

> Something that we
> Like to do.
> You read to me.
> I'll read to you.

Hop and Skip

I like to hop!

        I like to skip!

But sometimes
When I hop,
I trip.

        And sometimes
        When I skip,
        I slip.

        And sometimes then
        Our clothes might rip.

And when they rip,
My mom gets mad.

        And when they rip,
        So does my dad.

My mom says, "Walk
Instead of run."

        My dad does, too,
        But that's no fun.

        If you just walk
        To where you go,
        Instead of run,
        You go too slow.

But if you skip

        Or if you hop,

   Sometimes it's really hard
   To stop.

But sometimes it
Is nice to sit.

        Then let's sit down
        A little bit.

What shall we do?

        Now let me see.

   I'll read to you.
   You'll read to me.

The Snowman

Hi Ho! Hi Ho!
The world is white!

> Hi Ho! Hi Ho!
> It snowed last night!

It snowed while we
Were fast asleep.

> It's nice and high.
> It's very deep.

Put on your clothes,
The ones for snow.

> Pull on your boots
> And then let's go!

What shall we do
The first of all?

> Let's build a snowman.
> Roll a ball.

I'll roll the bottom
On the ground.

> I'll make the middle
> Nice and round.

I'll find a pebble
For each eye.

> And if he starts to melt,
> He'll cry!

His mouth can be
An apple slice.

An apple slice
Will turn to ice.

I'm getting pretty
Icy, too.

You do look icy.

So do you.

Let's go inside
And get a drink.

Some cocoa would
Be good,
I think.

And while we're in,
What shall we do?

You read to me.
I'll read to you.

The Dime

I found a dime!

           You found a dime?

I'm finding money
All the time.

           Where do you find it?

Here and there.
Along the street
And everywhere.

           I lost a dime.

You lost a dime?

           I'm losing money
           All the time.
           I wonder if
           You found *my* dime?

I found my dime
At dinnertime.

           I lost *my* dime
           At five o'clock
           When I was walking
           Down the block.

If what I found
Belongs to you,
There's just one dime
Instead of two.

Shall we divide
The dime in two?

A nickel each?
It's up to you.

Or shall we buy
One thing to share?

That would be fun.
That would be fair.

We could buy
A storybook.

We'll hold it so
We both can look.

We'll hold it so
We both can see.

I'll read to you.
You'll read to me.

I Like

I like soda.

I like milk.

I like satin.

I like silk.

I like puppies.

I like kittens.

I like gloves.

And I like mittens.

I like apples.

I like pears.

I like tigers.

I like bears.

I like to slide.

I like to swing.

We don't agree
On anything!

I like butter.

I like jam.

I like turkey.

I like ham.

I like rivers.

I like lakes.

I like cookies.

And I like cakes.

I like yellow.

              I like blue.

I like pizza.

              I like stew.

I like summer.

              I like spring.

        We don't agree
        On anything!

There's something else
I like a lot.
But if I like it,
You will not.

              There's something else
              That I like, too.
              But you won't like it
              If I do.

Tell me yours
And I'll tell mine.

              I like reading.
              Reading's fine!

You like reading?

              Yes, I do.

Why, reading was
What I picked, too!

              Well, then, at last
              We both agree!
              I'll read to you!
              You'll read to me!

My Snake

I have a snake.
Her name is Jill.
She sits upon
The windowsill.

You keep a snake
To be your pet?
A pretty scary pet,
I bet.

Jill isn't scary,
Not a bit.

But can she fetch
Or can she sit?

She hasn't learned
To do that yet,
But still she is
A perfect pet.

But can she beg
Or chase a ball?
Does she come running
When you call?

She cannot beg
Or chase or run.
But still Jill is
A lot of fun.

She doesn't sound
Like fun to me.
What can she do?
What fun is she?

Well, Jill can hiss
And Jill can smile

                    Your snake can smile?

Once in a while.
And Jill can shed
Her snaky skin.

                    She sheds her skin?
                    Then what's she in?

She's in another
Skin that's new.

                    Well, that's a clever
                    Thing to do.

And when I read
My favorite books,
Jill hangs around my neck
And looks.

                    A thing like that
                    I'd like to see.
                    Will Jill look at
                    Some books with me?

She'll do it
If I'm reading, too.

                    Well, then, I know
                    What we should do.

          You read to me!
          I'll read to you!

The Telephone

Ding-a-ling!

        Ting-a-ling!

(The telephone
Begins to ring.)

Hello!

        Hello!

Hello!

        Hello!

It's me.

        I know.
        It's me.

I know.
Are you in bed?

        Not yet. Are you?

I'm almost there.

        I'm almost, too.

I'm in pajamas.

        I'm not yet.
        I took a bath.
        My hair's still wet.

Did you do
The spelling list?

        I did. Did you?
        There's one I missed.

I missed two.
I had to look.

Have you read
The chapter book?

I've just started
Chapter three.

I have, too,
So read with me!

Read together,
Not alone,
While we're on
The telephone?

It won't take long
To get it done.

I'll get my book.
It sounds like fun.

Back and forth
Until we're through.

You read to me!
I'll read to you!

The Puppy

The puppy's muddy!
Look at her!

I've never seen
Such dirty fur!

My goodness,
She's a grubby pup!

I think we better
Clean her up.

Let's put the puppy
In the tub

And give the pup
A great big scrub

With lots of water,
Lots of soap,

And that will get her clean,
I hope.

Now rinse her off.
Her bath is done.

It's time to dry her
In the sun.

She looks so pretty,
All fluffed up.

I've never seen
So clean a pup!

Oops! Oh, my!
She got away!

She's in the mud!
Her coat is gray!

She's dirtier
Than yesterday!

She's having fun.
Let's let her play.

Then let's find
Something else to do.

I know what
And you do, too!

You read to me!
I'll read to you!

The Bear

My little brother
Saw a bear.

        He saw a bear?
        He saw it where?

He said he saw it
In his bed.
That's where it was,
My brother said.

        Your brother saw
        A bear in bed?
        In his own bed?

That's what he said.

        I bet it gave him
        Quite a fright!

It asked if it
Could spend the night.

        Spend the night
        Right in his bed?
        The bear asked that?

That's what he said.

        So then what did
        Your brother say?

He told the bear
That it could stay,
That it could stay
A night or more
If it would promise
Not to snore.

Your little brother
Sounds quite brave
To tell a bear
How to behave.

He said he fed it
From a cup.
(Sometimes he likes
To make things up.)

He made it up
About the bear?

Perhaps he did,
But I don't care.
It's still a story
That is fun.

Then let's make up
Another one.

We'll write it down
And when we're through
You'll read to me!
I'll read to you!

New Friends

My birthday's here!

> And mine is, too!

How old are you?

> How old are you?

I asked you first.
You've got to say.

> All right, I'm six.
> I'm six today.

Why, I am, too!
We're just the same!
We both are six!

> Well, what's your name?

Well, what is yours?

> You've got to tell.
> I asked you first.

It's Annabelle.

Now what is yours?

> Why don't you guess?

You've got to tell.

> All right, it's Jess.

Where do you live?

> I live quite near.
> Where do you live?

A block from here.

It's funny that
We've never met.
I've walked right by
Your house, I bet.

I bet I've walked
Right by yours, too,
And yet we never
Even knew.

Well, let's be friends.

I'd like that fine.

Now you're my friend.

And you are mine.

Do you know how to read?

Do you?

I asked you first.

I can.

Me, too.

Well, if we both can read,
Let's do!
You read to me!
I'll read to you!

The End

We're at the end

The very end

The very
Very
Very
End.

No more words

Or pictures. Look!

No more stories

In this book.

But there are other
Books to read.

Hundreds

Thousands

All we need.
Any time
In any weather
We can sit
Right down together.

In the shade

Or in the sun

Choose a book

That looks like fun.

One that's old

Or one that's new.

Make-believe

Or really true.

I'll read one line

I'll read two.

You'll read to me.
I'll read to you.

The End